REVEALED:
ZACK, WES, GRIZZ AND LUKE ARE SPRUNG BY
A SIZZLING MASTER PLAN FROM THE CLUB'S
NEW OWNER. STRAP IN AND GRIP TIGHT AS
THE 4 ACES ARE UNLEASHED.

·YA
1773845
3G

HIGHGATE ECHO *sport*

CHOPPER DAVIS IN SALAD SHOCK
NEW DIET, OLD TRICKS
SEE PAGE 50

SUPERCHEF COOKS UP WINNING RECIPE FOR COMETS SURVIVAL

Soccer world stunned as culinary billionaire takes over at Highgate

EXCLUSIVE
BY DARREN PHILIP AT HALEY STADIUM

Last-minute results don't come any closer than the **SHOCKING** events that unfolded last night at the Highgate Comets, when Britain's top menu-master **SNATCHED** a controlling stake in the club seconds before administrators were due to be called in.

Grateful fans of the Comets are already hailing it a **MIRACLE** and this morning thundering chants of "He did the deal, he cooks a posh meal…. He's the Chef, he's the Chef" were echoing around the normally restrained neighbourhoods of Highgate.

2

...EVEN ZACK AND JED STARTED GETTING ALONG!

THE WARRIORS FANS GET WARMED UP...

SLIGHTLY DIFFERENTLY FROM THE COMETS FANS...

THANK YOU, MR. JOSHUA! ARE YOU LOOKING FORWARD TO THE WARRIORS GAME?

YEAH, SOMETHIN' LIKE THAT...

C'MON, WES. WE BETTER GO. FLYING FIRST THING.

27

29

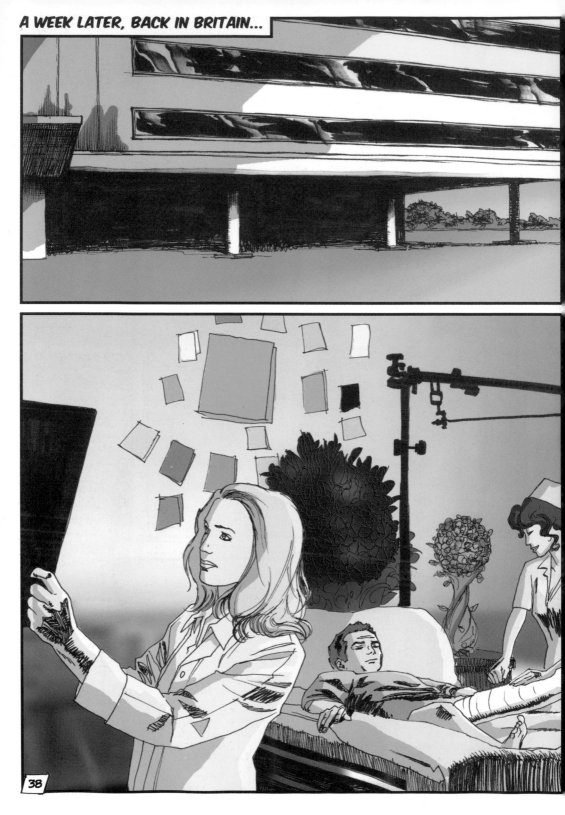

OUTSIDE...

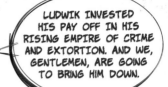

LUDWIK INVESTED HIS PAY OFF IN HIS RISING EMPIRE OF CRIME AND EXTORTION. AND WE, GENTLEMEN, ARE GOING TO BRING HIM DOWN.

HUH?!

LUDWIK USES THE WARRIORS AS A FRONT FOR HIS CORRUPT DEALINGS, THUGGERY AND CRIME EMPIRE.

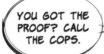

YOU GOT THE PROOF? CALL THE COPS.

AGREED, LUKE. WHAT ARE WE SUPPOSED TO DO?

I CAN'T LET YOU ENDANGER THE TEAM, CHEF. WE'RE JUST FOUR GUYS – AND WE'RE NOT TRAINED FOR THIS KIND OF WORK.

ALL'S NORMAL OUTSIDE LUKE'S PAD...

BUT INSIDE'S A DIFFERENT MATTER...

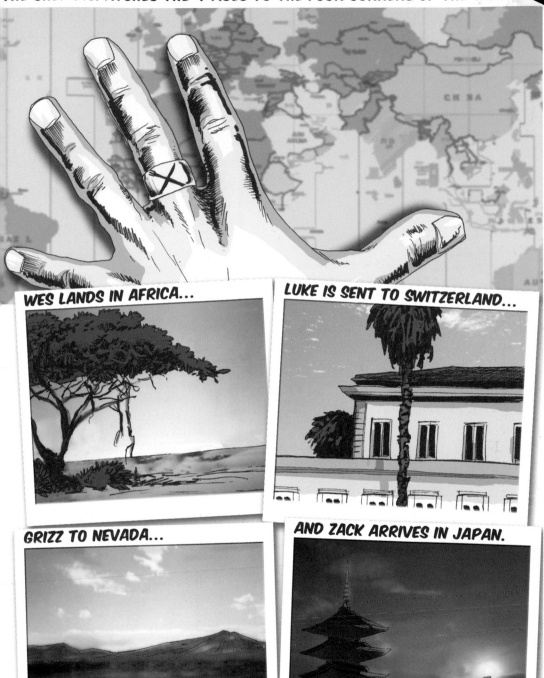

WES LANDS IN AFRICA...

LUKE IS SENT TO SWITZERLAND...

GRIZZ TO NEVADA...

AND ZACK ARRIVES IN JAPAN.

THE 4 ACES RETURN HOME FROM THEIR "TRAINING"...

CHANGED FOREVER!

IF I WAS A CROOKED REF, WHERE WOULD I HIDE?

I KNOW SOMEONE I CAN ASK.

ANYHOW, WHO SAYS HE'S HIDING?

GOOD POINT, WES.

CHECK CASINOS, TOP HOTELS AND CAR DEALERSHIPS.

ESS DENIED!

LET'S SEE WHO'S BEEN SHEDDING CASH.

87

97

99

105

WITH A LITTLE HELP FROM AN OLD FRIEND...

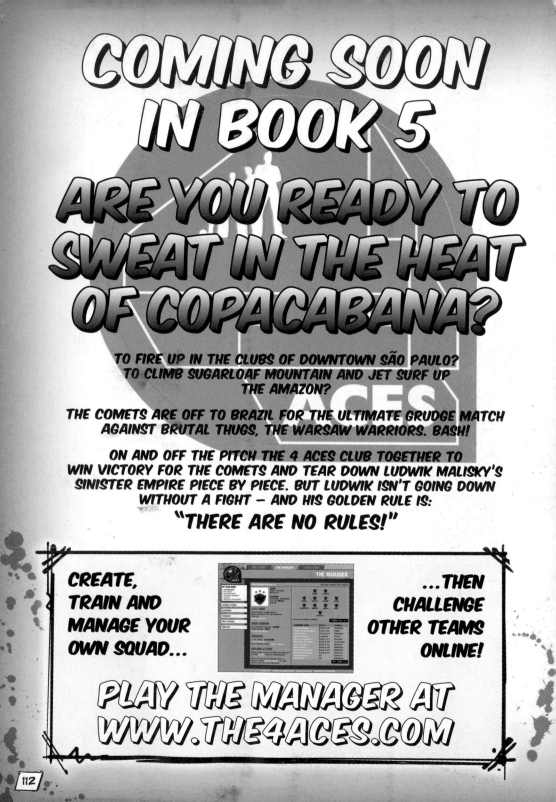